GWION AND THE WITCH

Jenny Nimmo

Jac Jones

This impression published in 2007 by Pont Books, an imprint of
Gomer Press, Llandysul, Ceredigion, SA44 4JL

First published in 1996; reprinted 1998, 2003.

ISBN 978 1 85902 294 8

A CIP record for this title is available from the British Library.

© Copyright text: Jenny Nimmo
© Copyright illustrations: Jac Jones

The author and illustrator assert their moral right under the
Copyright, Designs and Patents Act, 1988
to be identified respectively as author and illustrator of this work.

Printed and bound in Wales at
Gomer Press, Llandysul, Ceredigion

Once, long ago, there was a witch called Ceridwen. She was the wife of Tegid Foel, a nobleman, and they lived on the shores of Llyn Tegid, or Bala Lake. Ceridwen loved only one thing in the whole world— her son, Morfran. He was ugly and very stupid but Ceridwen dreamed that one day he would be the most brilliant boy in all Wales.

As years passed, Morfran showed no signs at all of becoming the wonderful boy that Ceridwen longed for. Every day he seemed to grow more hideous and foolish. Children ran away from him, dogs barked at him, and the villagers laughed secretly at his nonsense. No one dared to laugh out loud. They were afraid of being turned into frogs, or worse. For Ceridwen would roam the countryside with her black cat, listening at cottage doors and sometimes even changing her shape, so you could never be sure what or who she was.

'I fear for our poor son,' Tegid Foel said one day. 'He's an idiot. He'll never find a wife.'

Ceridwen was tempted to turn her husband into a donkey. 'How dare you say such a thing?' she said. 'Morfran will be famous, just you wait. I have found a spell in the books of the magician, Vergil of Toledo. It will give our son knowledge and understanding. If I cannot make Morfran beautiful, then I shall at least make him wise.'

Ceridwen ordered a great cauldron from the blacksmith, Gofannon, and when it was delivered she told Morfran, 'The cauldron is for you. I'm going to fill it with very special plants and herbs. We'll mix them with water from the lake and when the brew has simmered and been stirred for a year and a day, you must drink the first three drops that bubble out of it. But only three, my darling, for the rest will be poison.'

'Who says?' asked foolish Morfran.

'The magician, darling,' cooed Ceridwen.

'Who's going to stir the stuff, Mam?'

'Why, the blind man, Morda. He came begging your father for work only yesterday. He won't be able to see my magic brew and tell about it.'

Ceridwen suddenly realised that she would have to find someone to guide the old man, and to fetch sticks for the fire. I'll find someone who's used to hard work and not too inquisitive, she thought. An ordinary boy.

The boy Ceridwen chose was little Gwion from Llanfair Caereinion. Gwion was afraid of the tall woman who came peering into the house one hot summer day, but his mother welcomed her in.

'What can I do for your ladyship?' she asked, bowing her head.

'I want your son to work for me,' said Ceridwen. 'He shall be returned to you at the end of a year and a day.'

'We're honoured, gracious lady,' Gwion's mother said nervously, for no one ever refused a witch. 'Gwion, fetch your things and off you go. The w . . . the lady Ceridwen musn't be kept waiting.'

Ceridwen sailed away without a word of thanks, while Gwion wrapped up his few belongings. He was a cheerful boy, always on the lookout for adventure. 'Who knows,' he told himself, 'I may find my fortune.'

The animals were sad to see kind-hearted Gwion leave. 'Take care of Mam!' he called to them, as he hurried after the impatient witch.

It was dark in the barn where Ceridwen had hung her cauldron. This made no difference to Morda, of course, but poor Gwion wondered how long he would last in such a gloomy, stifling place.

Ceridwen had already filled the cauldron with lake-water, and now little Gwion had to keep it simmering. All day he toiled, carrying logs and sticks from the pile outside the barn and heaping them beneath the cauldron.

When Ceridwen was satisfied that Morda and Gwion were able to keep the water boiling, she flung the first handful of herbs into the cauldron and set off for the mountains, leaving Morfran to watch over the workers.

The witch was away every day from dawn to dusk. At night she would return with a basket of herbs and drop them, one by one, into the boiling liquid. Now, to add to the gloom and the heat, the barn was filled with wicked, pungent smells.

Autumn came, bringing a crop of fruit that had to be picked at its most potent. Ceridwen donned a feather cape and made for the windy orchards to collect her precious ingredients.

Winter arrived and howled round the barn like a pack of wolves. Sometimes snow drifted under the door, and the pile of logs grew heavy with ice. Ceridwen changed her feather cape for a thick fur coat and a hood lined with down. The winter berries and soggy mosses that she threw into

the cauldron made the water sizzle like a demon and Gwion reeled dizzily under his armful of logs. But if he stumbled or paused a moment to get his breath, he would feel Morfran's little stick in his back, 'Go on! Go on! Mam says you're not to stop.'

Spring was no better than winter. It was a harsh season that year. Frost sparkled on the hills and the mountain streams froze into bands of silver. Freezing mists slithered through the forests, and so did Ceridwen, intent on her task. She rooted for bulbs and scraped at lichen with her sharp nails, happily confident that Morfran would soon have all the wisdom that the earth could yield. 'He'll speak like an angel,' she promised herself. 'He will know every story ever told. His words will be poetry!'

At last, summer arrived. The crops in the valley grew waist-high and the fields were bordered with bright poppies and cornflowers as blue as the sky. Some days, Gwion would pause with his bundle outside the barn door. He would turn his face to the hills above Llanfair Caereinion and breathe deeply, filling his lungs with all the fresh sweet smells of summer. Would he never be free?

One night Ceridwen came in with a basket of very odd-looking roots. The stink they made was worse than all the other plants put together. Morda and Gwion choked on the vicious fumes and Morfran coughed until his eyes streamed.

'You run along to bed, my precious,' Ceridwen told him. 'Mam will see to things from now on.'

It was the beginning of the worst month of all for Gwion. Ceridwen had put in every ingredient the spell needed. Now, for one more month, the brew must be kept simmering at just the right temperature. Then it would be ready for Morfran to drink. All through that hot month of July, the witch never took her eyes off little Gwion. If he slackened for one second she would pull his ear, or stick her bony finger in his back, or kick his shins with her stiff leather shoe.

The last day dawned.

'Your work will be over tonight,' Ceridwen told Gwion and Morda. 'The brew is almost ready.'

'Ready for what?' asked Gwion, feeling brave now that he thought he would soon be going home.

'Never you mind,' snapped Ceridwen. She called Morfran and made him stand beside the cauldron.

'It's too hot,' whined Morfran, 'Why've I got to stand here?'

'You know very well,' hissed his mother. 'You must drink the first of the drops of the magic brew. Have you forgotten?' Ceridwen sighed irritably, then she smiled and stroked her son's cheek. Soon he would be wise. Soon he would understand everything. She could hardly wait.

The barn filled with a thick, acrid steam and Ceridwen felt her eyelids droop. How tired she was after her busy year. How she longed for a little nap. Her head sank onto her chest. 'No, I must watch,' she muttered, propping one eye open with her gnarled fingers.

The sun began to set but there was no relief from the heat. If anything, the temperature inside the barn was rising.

'I must rest,' groaned Morda. 'I can't go on.'

'Very well. You may sit down for five minutes,' said the witch. 'No longer, mind. Gwion, you stir.'

Gwion took the heavy spoon from Morda and drew it through the the bubbling liquid. It was definitely thicker now — a greasy, sticky concoction the colour of mud.

'Disgusting, isn't it?' said Gwion.

'Yeah!' agreed Morfran.

'Whatever does your Mam want it for?'

'I've got to drink it,' grunted Morfran.

'Rather you than me,' said Gwion. 'Are you ill or something?'

'Something, I suppose,' said Morfran, half to himself.

Gwion glanced into Ceridwen's corner. Her eyes were closed and she was breathing heavily. Perhaps he could take a break, a few seconds to ease his aching arms.

'Stir,' said Morfran, 'or I'll tell Mam.'

'Please don't,' begged Gwion. 'I've got cramp. I just want to rest for a second.'

At that moment the liquid began to gurgle. Huge bubbles rose to the surface. It looked like the face of a grinning monster.

'Ooooo!' gasped Gwion, dropping the spoon SPLASH into the cauldron. Three drops of boiling liquid flew out and onto his hand.

'Ooooowch!' he squealed, sucking his scalded fingers, and of course swallowing the magic drops.

In an instant little Gwion understood everything. He knew every story in the world: he knew how the stars were made and why the moon sailed through the sky. He also knew for sure that Ceridwen would try to kill him. Roused from sleep by the terrible commotion, she had guessed what had happened, and was even now rushing towards him.

'Help!' cried Gwion, running for the door.

But the witch was after him, her dreadful screech making Gwion's legs tremble. I wish I were a hare, he thought. Then I might escape her. And in that instant, he *was* a hare, racing towards the river. But now the witch was a hound with long muscled legs that were gaining on the hare with every bound. Gwion leapt for the river, wishing he were a fish, and he became one, twisting, turning, and darting through the water. But now the witch was an otter coming after him. SWISH! SWISH! She was drawing closer with her cruel otter's teeth.

Gwion leapt for the sky, wishing he were a bird, and he soared into the air, cloaked in feathers. But he couldn't escape Ceridwen. She was now a hawk with murderous talons.

Far below, Gwion spied a farmyard and he swooped down, wishing to be nothing more than a grain of wheat. Hidden among so many grains, surely Ceridwen would never find him. He dropped to the ground as the tiniest grain, but still he wasn't safe. There came towards him a sleek red hen with a scarlet crest. The witch had changed her shape again. She stared at the grain of wheat with her fierce green eye, she scratched it, pecked it—and swallowed Gwion whole.

But that was not the end of little Gwion. The seed of wheat grew inside the witch and at the end of nine months she gave birth to a beautiful baby boy. She knew who it was, of course, and was so angry she wanted to kill the child. But how could she?

For the first time in her life, Ceridwen didn't know what to do. She tore her clothes and raged through the mountains. Her groans became the thunder that shook the rocks and her tears the streams that foamed down the mountain-sides. It was a spring of terrible storms. The people of Bala wondered what would become of them if Ceridwen didn't simmer down. 'She is like her own wretched cauldron,' they muttered, 'ready to boil over and drown us all.'

Morfran was very jealous of the baby. 'You don't love me any more, Mam,' he cried. 'You love the baby better.'

'Not true!' Ceridwen told him. 'I love you, my precious. You are my true son.'

'Then kill the baby, Mam. Prove that you love me.'

Ceridwen looked at the mis-shapen boy she loved, and then she looked at the beautiful child she hated, and she made her decision. She couldn't kill the baby for he was filled with all the strength and wisdom that she had striven to create. She knew that she would never make anything as precious again. 'I cannot kill him, Morfran,' she said, 'for he belongs to the world. But you will never see him again.' And that night she sewed the baby into a leather bag and cast him into the sea.

Early next morning the tide carried the leather bag into the Dyfi estuary. The bag bobbed high on the waves and right over the weir at the mouth of the river. And when the tide turned, the little bag was trapped in the pool, instead of drifting out to sea.

From his leather cocoon the baby looked up at the brilliant sky. He saw ducks, a cloud, a spray of silver. He heard the lap of water all around him, and he remembered his strange flight from the witch. But where was he now? And who was he? What was his name? He certainly wasn't Gwion.

'Do you know who I am?' he asked the ducks.

They couldn't say.

The baby found that his head was full of poetry. He had so much to tell, and no one to talk to. What will become of all my wonderful words, he wondered. Will no one ever hear them?

Sitting beside the weir was a young nobleman named Elffin. He was the son of Gwyddno Garanhir and nephew of King Maelgwn of Gwynedd, but he was also a bit of a rascal, always getting into debt, always causing his father trouble. That morning, the first day of May, his father had told him he could keep all the fish caught in the weir to pay off his debts. 'After that, I wash my hands of you,' Gwyddno said.

There was usually a very good catch on Mayday but poor Elffin was having bad luck. There was not a single fish in the pool. And then he saw the leather bag. What could it be? A treasure?

Elffin drew the bag towards him and saw the baby's head peeping out. 'Taliesin!' Elffin exclaimed in Welsh, 'a fine forehead!'

'Taliesin!' echoed the baby. 'That also means *of great worth*. Let my name be Taliesin.'

Elffin lifted the baby out of the bag. 'You can talk!' he cried. 'Yet you are only a baby.'

'Oh, yes, I can talk,' said the baby Taliesin, and he told Elffin of his strange adventure.

As Elffin carried him home, Taliesin sang and told his tales. His words were poetry and Elffin listened, enchanted, to the baby's tuneful voice. His luck had changed at last. He had found a bard—and at that time bards were the most honoured men in the land, second only to a Prince.

'What a wonderful child you are,' said Elffin.

Ceridwen had worked the most powerful spell of her life and little Gwion had been at the centre of an adventure wilder even than his dreams. When Taliesin grew up to become the finest bard in Britain, there could be no doubt that the magic of their story would be told for years to come.